Books for E

Fire Fighter

By

My books are a project to get my son to enjoy reading. The stories use early reading words and subject matter young boys like. The words in the book range from pre-primer through third grade words. Early readers will find reading and learning more enjoyable because of the appropriate and interesting content.

For all boys who find reading boring!

Making Reading Fun!

© 2013 Marc Sevigny. All rights reserved.
ISBN 978-1-304-08653-2

Fire Fighter

"T.V. is so boring," I guess I will go outside and work on my tree house.

I was sawing some wood for my tree house. I took a rest and a big red fire truck went zooming by my house.

I climbed up the tree to get a better look. As the truck went by, my eyes closed. The alarm started ringing.

I quickly jumped into my fire truck and took off.

I arrived at the fire and put on my fire suit.

I sprayed water on the house
to put out the fire.

I got another call on the radio and had to go rescue someone from the water.

I ran to the helicopter for help.

I was lowered down to the water and said, "I will get you! Hang on!"

I put my hand out to the man and pulled him out of the water.

A new call came over the radio, "Floor seven on fire!" I had to move fast to my next rescue.

After a short ride on the fire truck, we stopped. I had to jump to the back and put up the long ladder. Then I started to climb.

I jumped off the ladder to look for people. I did not have to go far because they were already out of the building.

Another call came on the radio, "Car on fire!" We went back down the ladder to get into the fire truck.

The car was on fire with orange and red flames. I was able to put the fire out and did not hurt myself.

Today was a very busy day being a fire fighter. I backed the truck into the fire house. My mom started calling for me as my eyes opened. I smiled and said, "Good! Time for lunch!"

The End

Keep Reading!

More Books from Mr. 7 Yea!

The Hunter

Cowboy

Runaway Sailboat

Cool Forts

The Fish that Ate Me

Lost Campers

Baseball Wars

Dinosaurs

My Rocket Ship